THiS PLACE iS NOT MY HOME

Cyn Bermudez

An imprint of Enslow Publishing

WEST **44** BOOKS™

BROTHERS

TAKEN AWAY · NOT HOME FOR THE HOLIDAYS

THIS PLACE IS NOT MY HOME · JUST MAYBE

Please visit our website, www.west44books.com. For a free color catalog of all our high-quality books, call toll free 1-800-542-2595 or fax 1-877-542-2596.

Cataloging-in-Publication Data

Names: Bermudez, Cyn.
Title: This place is not my home / Cyn Bermudez.
Description: New York : West 44, 2019. | Series: Brothers
Identifiers: ISBN 9781538382318 (pbk.) | ISBN 9781538382325 (library bound) | ISBN 9781538383162 (ebook)
Subjects: LCSH: Foster home care--Juvenile fiction. | Electronic mail messages--Juvenile fiction. |
Siblings--Juvenile fiction.

First Edition

Published in 2019 by
Enslow Publishing LLC
101 West 23rd Street, Suite #240
New York, NY 10011

Editor: Theresa Emminizer
Designer: Sam DeMartin

Printed in the United States of America

CPSIA compliance information: Batch #CS18W44: For further information contact Enslow Publishing LLC, New York, New York at 1-800-542-2595.

BROTHERS

⟨HAPTER ONE
How Far Is the Moon?

From: victory333@email.com
To: isaac-the-great@email.com
Subject: the new foster keepers

I listened to records today. Do you remember what they are? Momma would play them when she cleaned house. Dad when he fixed cars. Momma used to have a bunch. Said they were "retro." She got rid of them when Dad died. You were five, halfway to six. I was seven. Records are how music was played in the olden days.

My new foster keepers collect records. They have shelves full of them. I listened to Momma's favorite song: "Moon River." Ugh…I used to hate that song. But I really wanted to hear it today. You know how rice reminds you of Momma? That song reminds me of Momma. It made my chest hurt, but I'd listen to it again if I could.

Listening to music was nice, even though I missed Momma. We don't get to do much around here. There are a lot of us. So it can get crazy here.

My new foster keepers are real strict. They call it "controlled chaos." They have rules for everything! They have rules for the house. For us kids. For the things we share. Even for the few things that are our own.

Brian and Amy are my keepers. They live a few blocks from my first keeper, Ms. Cutter. At least I'm still at the same school with Lucky.

There are six of us kids. Mason, Rockford, and I are in one room. The girls, Cora, Boots, and Megs, are in another. Cora is the oldest. She's 16. Mason is the youngest, just five.

You should see this house! It's big and old and smelly. There are always noises. Usually one of the kids is making noise. Or Feather is singing (she's a bird). Or Boom is barking (he's a dog). But when it's supposed to be quiet, it's not. The floorboards creak whenever it's silent. It creaks the most at night when everyone is asleep. The paint outside and inside the house is peeling. I can hear the train rumbling by every night. It whistles so loud I think the house might fall apart one day.

But that's nothing compared to the way the wind whines. The way it rustles the old tree branches outside the bedroom window. The way it howls during a full moon. The way it sounds, some nights, like a woman crying. Mason thinks he sees shadows. He's always hiding under the covers at bedtime. Brian says the house is just settling. I don't believe him.

Sometimes, I'm glad for all the rules and chores. I don't have time to get too scared! Or let my imagination run away like last time…

All of us kids are cooking or cleaning, or we're at school. Lights out is the same for all of us. I'm usually so tired by the end of the day. We get an hour of free time. I'm glad they have a laptop. It takes forever to turn on, but it works. I'm going to email Lucky, too. Sometimes I sit out in the yard with Boom. He's my favorite. Brian and Amy have a bunch of pets:

- Boom Box – He's a gray boxer.

- Socks – He's an orange cat.

- Schrodinger – She's a black cat.

- Feather Fawcett – She's a yellow and white bird.

- Pork Chop – He's the goldfish. Actually, we don't know if he's a boy or a girl. I think he's a boy.

That's why Brian and Amy are "frugal," because there are a lot of mouths to feed. That's what Amy said. Momma would have called them cheap. They buy everything "no name." Like soap is just called soap. Not named soap, like how Momma would buy Zest. Anyway, it's okay I guess. Brian said it's just as good as anything named.

The other kids don't talk to me much. I don't

care that they don't. I'm perfectly fine with Boom. The other kids know about Momma, too. One of them said something to me. It got nipped quickly because of the Conduct Rules.

Amy said Momma's crime made big news throughout the whole county. No one has ever tried to steal that much money before. From all those rich people she cleaned for. She said me, you, and our sisters will always be affected by what Momma did. She said it was a shame. I told her I was not ashamed of Momma. Then I got in trouble for talking back.

That was why I couldn't email you when I first got here. Anyway, one of the kids, Rockford, called me a thief like Momma. He said he heard thieving runs in the family. Said stuff started disappearing when I got here. Stuff like food or car keys. But now one of the records is missing! Brian and Amy haven't said anything about it. What if they think I took it? Well, I didn't.

Anyway, my hour is up.

TTYS
Victor

3 Attachments
Moon-River-45.jpg
Old-House.jpg
Boom.jpg

CHAPTER TWO
Not Such a Hollow World

From: isaac-the-great@email.com
To: victory333@email.com
Subject: The school play!

Whoa, that's a lot of pets! I'd forget all their names. Boom is cute, though. I wish John and Susan got a dog instead of a cat. Susan named the cat Ms. Penelope. She's a cool-looking cat. Ms. Penelope has blue eyes and white fur. She just sleeps and sleeps. Or she chases her shadow. Sometimes she sits on my lap.

I'm glad you didn't fight with anyone. Fighting caused me a big mess. I don't want you to have a big mess like me. But I'm also glad you stuck up for Momma. I just wish you hadn't got in the trouble you did. At least you didn't have to see the caseworker. I probably wouldn't have said anything. Susan and John don't talk about Momma like that. John told the other foster kid here, Eric, not to be mean. He said, "How would you feel if Isaac said something like that to *you?*"

I never thought about it before. Eric is in foster care, too. Something happened with his parents, just like ours. Just like that kid Rockford. Just like all the foster kids. Susan said most people aren't bad people. She said some people just make bad choices. Like Momma.

So Eric has backed off. He doesn't tease me anymore. Well, I guess he just doesn't tease me about Momma. He still calls me names. Sometimes he calls me twerp or nerd.

The kids at school don't bother me as much now. Things are better for me. I was worried I'd never get past what happened. How I punched that popular kid. Other kids talk to me now, not just Stephanie. But I only hang out with Stephanie at lunch. I like it that way. She does, too. We have a secret handshake now. Stephanie made it up. I told her I wanted to show you. She said I can. She said we can use her mom's phone to record a video. We'll do it on Monday.

Victor…I'm sorry about what happened. How Ms. Cutter sent you away after the werewolf thing. And now your new foster keepers…

I think you'd like it here. I think you'd like living with Susan and John. And if we're both here together…it won't be like being with Momma. But we'd be together at least. I wish you could be here right now.

Remember what our caseworker said? A foster home must have room. John and Susan only had room for one. But then Eric came back to them and there were two. And now John and Susan said they might have room for one more!

fingers crossed =D

I already asked if they can choose you. John said of course. I'm so excited!

Thank you for the pictures. I think I might remember Momma's records. How do you play the music on the record? I do remember "Moon River." Momma would sing it when she got ready to go out.

John's old Polaroid broke. So I don't have a camera right now. John said he'd fix the camera soon. I can still scan though. I wanted to show you this flyer. It's for the school play!

AUDITIONS!!!

Tom Sawyer
Thursday, October 13th
3:30–5:30
Auditorium

Come prepared to read from script!

Do you think I can do it? Susan said just believe in myself. She said reach for the moon. Dinner is ready! I gotta go.

TTYS

~Isaac

P.S. Do you think it's a ghost making all that noise? Stephanie thinks it might be a ghost. Remember the story Momma used to tell us on Halloween? About the woman who cries at night?

P.P.S. October is Momma's favorite month! Do you have a costume yet? I do. I'm a hamburger! Weird, huh? But kind of funny at the same time.

1 Attachment

Tom_Sawyer.jpeg

CHAPTER THREE
The Adventures of Victor and Isaac

To: victory333@email.com
From: isaac-the-great@email.com
Subject: There's a ghost in the house!

I remember the story Mom told: "La Llorona." The Lady in White. We used to get so scared. But it was fun, too. You would hide under the blankets.

Momma was good at telling us that story. She'd wear that dress she found at the Goodwill. The white one with puffy shoulders. She'd chase us around the living room. She would put her hands up with her fingers curled. She would shriek and weep and whine.

Lucky emailed me this link:

http://www.it's-a-ghost-folk-lore.com/ [author-tales-lady-in-white-24.htm](http://www.it's-a-ghost-folk-lore.com/author-tales-lady-in-white-24.htm)

"Have you seen the Lady in White? She stands by the water and weeps. Searching, searching…where are her children? Beware of La Llorona! She will pay the river's ransom if she finds you wandering alone." – Author Tales, an excerpt.

In Momma's version, it was a lake instead of a river. She said it was Lake Ming. We used to go there in the summer. There is an audio clip, too. Listen.

♫ Weeping Lady ▶

Creepy, huh!

Sounds like the wind. Sounds like what I hear at night.

Lucky said I should research the house. I asked how. He said, "Go to the library."

So I'm going to skip school. Don't worry. Just once. I'm just going to the library. Researching will take time. I'll need a whole day. Lucky is going with me. He's been practicing signatures. He'll write our sick notes. No one will find out. I promise.

Try out for the play. For sure! Of course you can do it. I wish I could be there with you.

I read *Tom Sawyer* last year in English. Tom and Huck run away together. Sorry for the spoiler. I won't say any more! I only mention it because sometimes I can't stand it here. Sometimes I wanna leave this place.

Thank you for asking Susan and John. If I do get to stay there, then things won't be so bad. Really, anywhere is better than this place. And us together…well, that would be second-best. Being with Momma and Vanessa and Sara would be first-best.

The other kids in the house still aren't talking to me. They're always quiet when I walk into a room. Even Mason! Rockford and I go to the same school. Now kids at my school know. I don't have it as bad as you did. Even though Rockford said I was taking stuff in the house.

Lucky is cool about it. Lucky knows I don't steal. Same with our other friends. But they do joke around. They gave me a nickname. They call me Twist. As in Oliver Twist, the orphan boy who lives with thieves. I don't say anything. I laugh, but I don't mean it. I don't like the nickname. Mostly because I'm not an orphan!

We are not orphans. Dad is dead, but Momma will be home soon. Lucky is the only one who doesn't call me Twist.

Anyway. I'm already tired, and the sun is

still out. I just got home from school. My free time is now. The older kids have free time from 7:30 to 8:30. Dinner must be ready by 6:00, dishes clean by 7:30. Bedtime is 8:30, no exceptions.

Right now, I have to cut green beans and peel potatoes. Then it's my turn to clean the kitchen. And it's my turn to help Mason with his homework. I have my own homework to do!

My free time is almost up. I wanted to email Lucky, too. We can't even watch TV unless all the kids agree on a show. I don't even bother!

TTYS
Victor

P.S. No costume yet! I have to find a way to get one on my own.

1 Attachment
Weeping-Lady.mp3

CHAPTER FOUR
Tetherball Fiasco

From: isaac-the-great@email.com
To: victory333@email.com
Subject: Getting ready for Halloween!

There's a new kid being teased at school. His name is Marty. He's not new to the school. The kids have teased him before. He's kind of a know-it-all. Stephanie said he's a loudmouth. He's always correcting everyone. If you don't say something right. Or if you do math wrong.

We have science together. But he's smart and

dumb at the same time! He's real smart at knowing school stuff. But he's clumsy. He's always walking into things. Last week, he ran into a pole. He was playing tetherball. He missed the ball. The rope that tethers the ball to the pole wrapped around him. He tripped over his feet and ran into the pole.

Everyone used to call him Smartie Marty. They'd toss those Smarties candies at him. The ones we always got trick-or-treating. Now they're calling him Trippy. Or Sir Trippy. Or Sir Trips-A-Lot. That's why I stay away from the tetherball. I might end up doing the same thing!

At least you're not Marty. Your friends believe you. Plus, you *have* friends! I know you're not a thief. Has anything else gone missing?

I've been practicing for the audition. Stephanie has been helping me. I'm trying out for the part of Huck Finn. Stephanie reads Tom's part. The audition is in two parts. First we do a scene alone. Then we do a scene with one other person. I'm so nervous! My stomach aches.

I've been real busy getting stuff ready for Halloween. Susan's church is having a party. I'm helping. I'm stuffing the treat bags. There are 100 treat bags in all. I wish I could help you with your chores. I have to keep my room clean. But I have a lot of time for myself. I can watch TV after my homework is done. Eric and I take turns picking the TV shows we watch.

I can't believe you don't have a costume yet! Momma made good costumes. All four of us would have matched in some way. Remember that one year when we did characters from *The Wizard of Oz*? I was the lion. You were the tin man. Vanessa was the scarecrow. And Sara was Dorothy. Momma was the witch. She even painted herself green.

We got a lot of candy that year. Everybody loved our costumes.

Susan and John are dressing up as ketchup

and mustard. Eric is dressing up as a hot dog. I thought being a burger was a good idea.

It fits the theme. Don't you think? It's not as fun without you and Momma and our sisters. Plus Momma's ideas were way better. But I think it's kind of funny. You should pick a costume soon. Maybe you and Lucky can match? Will you be able to go trick-or-treating? I hope so.

Oh yeah…DON'T SKIP SCHOOL!

What if you get caught? It's bad enough that you only get an hour a day. What if your foster keepers take that away from you? What if they send you away? They're worse than Ms. Cutter. You could end up with someone *way* worse!

Stephanie said you could get suspended. She said making fake sick notes was super bad. She said use your time wisely. If you don't, researching could take days.

Stephanie knows because she likes to research things. Just because she likes to know things. When she gets curious about something, she reads up on it. She said just know what you're looking for. She said first, you can always ask the librarian. She said you can use the index. Look for historical records and maps. Then search the newspapers.

Okay, to recap, here is the list:

- know what you want to look for
- use the index
- look for historical records
- check out old maps
- search the newspapers
- ask the librarian

I'm going to play practice now. Love you!

~ Isaac

P.S. Pick a costume!

CHAPTER FIVE
Exploring the Neighborhood

From: victory333@email.com
To: isaac-the-great@email.com
Subject: I drew a map.

There is a river that runs through the edge of town. It's only a few blocks from where I live. Lucky and I were checking out the neighborhood. He saw it first. Then he pointed it out to me. I forgot about that long river. The one that runs through the county. Seeing it gave me goosebumps.

I thought of La Llorona. Lucky reminded

me that the river runs near Lake Ming. But I think it's a different ghost in the house. It's still creepy, though. It made me wonder. But Lucky said the Lady in White is a legend. He said people tell it all over the world.

Anyway. Things keep going missing. We are allowed to own three items. I just have Dad's old camera. Luckily, it hasn't gone missing. Rockford's signed baseball is gone. He'd gotten it from an uncle. They still can't find Brian's keys. And now Cora's locket is gone! More and more, I think it's a ghost. A tricky one. A thief.

Of course, everyone in the house thinks it's me. Rockford repeats what he said before: things started going missing when I arrived. At first, the keepers didn't say anything. I figured they didn't believe Rockford. Now Amy asked me if I took anything. She said I wouldn't be in trouble. She said she understood because of Momma. I didn't like that. It made me so mad. But I learned my lesson. I didn't dare say anything back to her.

All I said was no. I didn't take anything. I don't think she believed me. Brian just gives me a look. Sort of like he is disappointed. I feel awkward in this house.

I don't want you to worry. I already skipped school. It was after my last email to you. That's when we checked out the neighborhood. We thought a test run was a good idea. Lucky wrote our notes. It's okay. We got away with it! Besides, I'm going stir-crazy here. Amy is keeping a closer eye on me. She's giving me more to do. Like I have to help Mason with his homework Monday through Friday. I have to do yard work and help in the kitchen every day, too.

I overheard Brian and Amy talking about the computer. They might take it away! THAT CANNOT HAPPEN! It just can't. The computer is the only thing I have here. It's the only way I can communicate with you. I'm not sure exactly what they were saying. I only heard the words "computer" (a few times) and "remove."

Anyway. I've been stressed. Hanging out with Lucky is the only break I've had. Exploring the neighborhood was needed. It was fun too. I drew a map. I snapped a picture of it.

We're going to the library next. I took your friend's advice. I'm prepared for the library. I know the "lay of the land," as Momma would say.

Don't worry. I'll talk with you soon.

Love you too!
Victor

P.S. That was my favorite Halloween. Momma played a good witch. Don't be a burger! Let's be zombies instead. You and I can still do a theme. That's what I pick. Zombies.

P.P.S. I don't have money for a costume. But this one will be easy to make. Lucky has Halloween makeup from last year. He said I can have it.

    P.P.P.S. I found this site about how to do zombie makeup: http://www.happy-halloween-fun.com/the-best-zombie-make-up-ever.htm

2 Attachments

Neighborhood-Map.jpg

Zombie-Costume.jpg

CHAPTER SIX
Kuya

From: isaac-the-great@email.com
To: victory333@email.com
Subject: I have good news and bad news.

    John said I should always give the good news first. He didn't say why. He said he likes the good news first. I can't ask you ahead of time. So I'll just give you the good news first.

    I got the part! Can you believe it? I'm going to play Huck Finn. You'll never guess who's playing the part of Tom. It's Jake. The kid I punched. The one who called Momma a bad name. The one who told everyone in school what Momma did. I was afraid he'd say something mean. He didn't say anything to me. He didn't even look at me. Not until it was time for our scenes. He ignores me when our scenes are over. It's weird.

I got there late, too. I was so nervous the night before. I had trouble sleeping. Then when I got there, I couldn't find the audition. I thought it was going to be in the auditorium. It wasn't. It was in the gym. I sat on the bleachers and waited for my turn. When I started reading my scene, it just… fell into place. I remembered my lines.

Another cool thing happened. I met someone new. A girl. Her name is Katie. She's in the play. She's got dark hair, like a raven. Her eyes match her hair. I like her smile. She's nice to me. At least when we talk. But that doesn't happen often. I think about her a lot. Sometimes I walk near her. But I don't know what to say. Except for hi, hello, how are you…I basically say the same thing. Do you think she'll think it's weird if I say hi to her in Filipino? I know. Yes, it's weird.

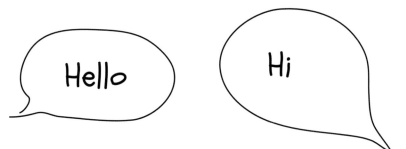

Hello

Hi

I've been learning Filipino words. It's actually called Tagalog. Susan and John have been teaching me. I learned a new Filipino word today. I mean Tagalog. "Kuya" means "brother." You say it like KOO-YA.

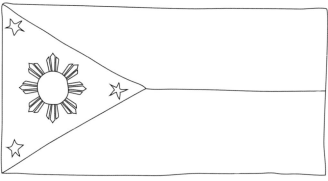

flag of the Philippines

"Ate" (AH-TEE) means "sister." Susan said it would be proper for me to call you kuya.

I wish I could say more to Katie. I want to ask her what she likes to do for fun. Like, does she like skating? Or reading? What's her favorite book? Does she like going to the movies? If she does, what movies does she like? What about music and food? What's a good way to start a conversation?

John said to just say hi to her. I have! He said just talk to her. I don't know what that means. I can't "just talk to her." He said to ask you what you would do. When he said that, I remembered the bad news. I knew I had to tell you.

The bad news is really sad news. You can't live here. Susan and John said they were about to say yes. But then something happened. They wouldn't tell me what it was. They just said an "unexpected change has occurred."

They said it was not the time for a new foster kid. I cried when they told me. I don't understand.

They were getting a
room ready.

I've been worried
about you, too. I don't
want you to get into more
trouble sneaking around.
But I know the house
history is important to
you. Did you find out
anything at the library?

Stephanie said you can help the ghost leave.
That doesn't sound true. I think Stephanie makes
up stuff sometimes.

I don't see how knowing anything about
the house will help you. I'm sorry, Victor. I wish I
could change things. But I can't.

~Isaac

P.S. John fixed his Polaroid.

P.P.S. I'm going to be a zombie with you!

I told Susan. She is buying the costume tomorrow.

1 Attachment

Tom-Sawyer.jpg

CHAPTER SEVEN
The River on the Moon

From: victory333@email.com
To: isaac-the-great@email.com
Subject: Congrats!

Yes! Good job. I'm happy for you, Isaac. You're going to be *great* in that part. You know what? You deserve it. I'm glad things are better for you. I really am.

I just want you to be safe and happy. I hope Vanessa and Sara are okay, too. Just don't forget about Momma. Be happy. Have fun. But this situation with you and Susan and John is temporary. We will all be back together soon. Me, you, Momma, and our sisters.

Don't be sad about me not living there. I didn't have much hope for it. Us being together right now was too good to be true. Susan and John probably have a good reason. So don't worry about it. Don't worry about me either.

Besides, Susan and John are good for you. That doesn't mean they're good for me. But I'm glad you tried. Momma would be glad, too.

I want you to be careful around Jake. Don't trust him. Jake is a bully. Maybe he's moved on. I hope so. Just keep your distance. Only talk to him when you have to. Like for the play.

I have sort of good news and sort of bad news, too. I'll follow what you did. Good news first. Things have been better with the other foster kids. It started with Megs. She saw me taking pictures. She asked me about the camera Dad left me. I showed her the photos I like to take. She liked them. Then she asked if I wanted to play Monopoly with her and Boots.

Megs and Boots are my age. Normally, I'd say no. But I hate everyone ignoring me. So I said yes. Turned out it was a lot of fun. Then Cora helped me with a math problem. She likes math. Cora thought I was a thief because the "Moon River" record went missing. But I told her I didn't take it.

Cora said, "But you're the only one who liked the song. Besides Brian and Amy."

I said, "Ew! I don't like that song. I only wanted to hear it because my mom loves the song. Hearing it made me sad."

Then Cora said, "Oh! We thought you took it."

"*We?*" I said.

"Me and Rockford," she said.

Now she nods hi to me. Even Rockford is

cool now. Cora must have told him what I said. Though, he can still be mean at times. Like when he calls me Twist. On Saturday night, we all played Monopoly. Even the keepers! I actually had a lot of fun. We even laughed.

Lucky and I went to the library on Monday. We spent the whole day there. I almost missed the bus back home. I would have hated being late. I would've gotten in big trouble. I would've been grounded for at least two weeks! That would have sucked big time.

Anyway. The sort of bad news is we didn't learn much at the library. The house is super old.

We already knew that. The house seems like it's falling down. Really!

The house was built in the 1920s. It changed owners four times. But we couldn't find if anyone died in the house. Lucky said it doesn't rule out a ghost in the house. Especially since the house *is* old. With all that time, anything could have happened.

I didn't tell Cora my idea about a ghost being the thief. I mean, they just started talking to me. Last thing I need is for them to start calling me weird, too. Weirdo Twist. Ugh!

Maybe it *is* La Llorona crying at night. But then who is taking stuff around the house? Lucky and I have a plan. We are going to catch whoever is taking the stuff. A ghost? La Llorona? Rockford? The last one is Lucky's guess. Lucky thinks Rockford is mean because he's really the thief.

"How'd you figure that?" I said. He just shrugged and said, "I just do. It's called a gut feeling."

He said it's like detectives in crime movies. The detectives follow a hunch, a gut feeling.

Anyway. Here's our plan:

- Skip last period. I have gym and Lucky has study hall. We won't miss much.

- Get to my keepers' house an hour early. Lucky sneaks in.

- Set up a hidden camera in the living room (Lucky's dad's camera).

- Wait and see.

Since it's Friday, Lucky told his parents he's spending the night. I'll sneak him into the closet. No one ever goes in there until morning. Our dirty school clothes go into the hamper in the bathroom. Our pajamas are in the drawers.

In the morning, I'll pretend to go to school. I'll have to ride the bus with Megs and Boots. Lucky will download the video. He'll do it once everyone leaves in the morning. By the time I get back to the house, it will be all done.

Good plan, huh? Foolproof.

:)

Gotta go. Lights out soon.

TTYS

Victor

1 Attachment

Monopoly.jpg

CHAPTER EIGHT
"Miracle Baby"

From: isaac-the-great@email.com
To: victory333@email.com
Subject: I'm sick.

I didn't go to school today. Can you believe it? I never miss school. Never. I don't like to, even when I'm sick. Right now, I'm super sick. I have a bad cold. My stomach was hurting. Earlier, I had trouble breathing. Susan took me to the doctor.

The doctor said I had a panic attack. He asked Susan if I had a lot of stress. He said the stress could make me sick. Susan said she didn't think so. I didn't say anything. I was too scared to. A lot of things stress me, Victor! A lot. Like Jake. Maybe he will turn on me like you said. Or I think about the kids being mean to me again.

Practicing for the play stresses me, too. I'm afraid I'll mess up. I'm afraid of totally and completely embarrassing myself. I'm afraid of embarrassing myself in front of Katie. Or really, just talking to Katie.

I worry about you, too. I worry about you all the time. I worry you're going to get caught. I don't like you skipping school. I worry about everyone thinking you are a thief. :(

I have a bad feeling about this. *A gut feeling.* About you and Lucky trying to catch the thief. What if it *is* a ghost? How are you going to get *that* on video? How will it help anything?

You know what else? Susan and John are having a baby. They are calling it a miracle.

Susan's doctor had said she wasn't able to have children. John said, "Foster care helps kids who need it most."

Now I'm afraid they will send me away. They don't need Eric or me anymore. They'll have their own kid soon. Maybe we *should* go. Like run away together. Like Tom and Huck. We can pretend we died. We can use the zombie makeup.

I know we can't. I just wish we could.

Stephanie said I shouldn't think about stuff too much. She said her dad thought about stuff too much. She said he got a hole in his stomach because of it. I don't want a hole!

Halloween is tomorrow! Are you ready? Susan said I have to stay home. I was gonna go trick-or-treating with Stephanie. We had the whole day planned. Now it's ruined.

I'm having the worst day ever!

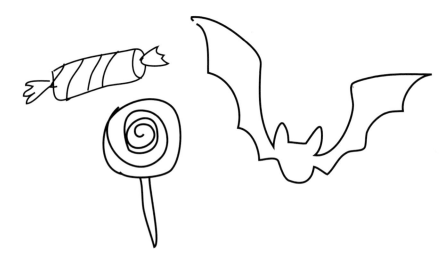

I have to get to bed now.

Love,

~Isaac

P.S. I hope you're okay.

P.P.S. You haven't emailed me all week.

P.P.P.S. The play is in two weeks! What if I'm not better by then? The part will go to someone else, an understudy.

P.P.P.P.S. :'(

CHAPTER NINE
A Twisted Halloween

From: victory333@email.com
To: isaac-the-great@email.com
Subject: Re: I'm sick.

I'm sorry, Isaac. I don't want you to worry. Why do you think Susan and John will get rid of you? Why would they do that? You always worry over everything.

Remember when Momma would say, "When it pours, have faith"? I've been thinking about that lately. I think she meant things can go wrong all at once. When they do, believe it will get better. We need to believe right now.

I have to tell you what happened. I don't want to. Especially with how sick you're getting. But you need to know. And you need to be brave.

You were right about your bad feeling. My plan didn't work.

At first, things went fine. It was on Halloween day. I left school. I met Lucky around the corner from the house. We went into the house and set up the camera. Then we waited. No one was supposed to be home for a while. Brian and Amy were at work. The kids were at school.

But then Brian came home early. Lucky and I went out the back. We decided to go back to school. Since our plan was ruined. We thought no one knew we skipped part of school. I didn't know Brian went to the school to pick me up early. He got there before I did. He was in a car. I was on a bus. Well, of course, I wasn't there. The school nurse showed Brian the note Lucky wrote. I didn't know any of this yet. I went to the rest of my classes. Then I went home.

Amy was waiting for me. She told me to sit in the den. We waited for Brian.

When Brian got home, they first asked me about school. I didn't lie. I told them I skipped. I told them I was researching the house. How a ghost might be haunting the place. I told them about La Llorona. I don't think they believed me. Brian's face was red. Amy wouldn't look at me. They were so angry.

Then more was said. Something bad happened when I was at school. More stuff is missing. I told you how the "Moon River" record went missing. At least, it's not in its sleeve on the shelf. Now they don't believe me that I didn't take it. They think I'm lying. A money clip disappeared from the keepers' bedroom. They blamed me! It was a lot of money, too. More than $300!

Amy kept asking me, "Where's the money?"

I said, "I don't know!" I said it over and over. Every time they asked me.

I was scared. They sent me to my room.

Rockford said I could go to juvie. Do you know what that is? Juvenile hall. It's like a jail, but for kids. I didn't do anything wrong. I didn't steal anything! It didn't matter what I said. Brian and Amy didn't believe me. They called the caseworker. She was coming to get me the next day. I ran away!

It was late. But I knew I needed to leave before morning. I left at night. I took Boom with me. He wanted to come. He kept barking and barking. If I hadn't taken him, he would have woken up the place. I went to Lucky's. But as I was walking up, I saw him. He was by his bedroom window. He signaled for me to leave. Amy and Brian had called his mom and dad. I had nowhere else to go. It was cold. I searched for an open car. I found one and slept in it. I left the car before sunrise.

I figured I'd go to the library. That way I could email you. I'm not leaving you behind. I'm going to come and get you. Send me your address? I'll wait here until I get it.

Didn't I say not to trust your keepers? Now look what happened. They're having a baby. Maybe they won't get rid of you and Eric. Maybe they will. Either way, you're not waiting around to find out.

I'm 30 minutes from you by car. That's about two hours by bus. Hurry up with the address!

Okay. Talk to you soon!

Love you,
Victor

P.S. The library closes at 6:00. If I don't hear from you by then, I'll go to the mall. I'll check my email at one of the computer stores.

1 Attachment

ghost-books-research-at-the-library.jpg

⟨HAPTER TEN
The Sun Always Rises

From: isaac-the-great@email.com
To: victory333@email.com
Subject: I hope you're okay.

Victor, I was going to go with you. I will always choose you. I will always choose our family, our mom, and our sisters. *Always.* I was packing my stuff. Then the caseworker called Susan and John! She asked if you were here. Then Susan asked me if you said anything to me. I didn't say anything. I kept quiet. I didn't mean to cry. I was strong. Then

John read our emails! They knew you ran away.

I couldn't email you right away. I would have warned you. Susan and John won't tell me what happened. They just said that I'll know soon. They said not to think about it. I can't help it!

I hope you're not in juvie. I know you didn't steal anything. I emailed Lucky. I asked if he heard anything. He said no.

Stephanie told me to pray. I said I didn't know how. She showed me. She said, "Just say thank you for what you have and say what you hope for." I asked her how she knew if God was listening. She said God always listens. I said I'm still not sure about God. She said I didn't need to be sure. She said prayer is for everyone.

I thought about what you said. About having faith that things will get better. Momma would want us to have hope. So I prayed. I've been praying every night.

Things have gotten better. I'm not sick

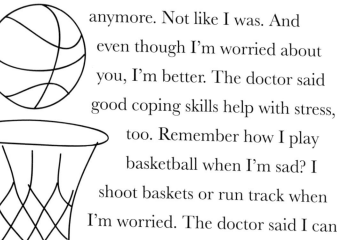

anymore. Not like I was. And even though I'm worried about you, I'm better. The doctor said good coping skills help with stress, too. Remember how I play basketball when I'm sad? I shoot baskets or run track when I'm worried. The doctor said I can do that when I'm mad, too. Not just when I'm sad or anxious.

You should try it. You don't have to play basketball. Remember how you and Dad used to play soccer? We'd go to games all the time. Momma would cheer. Vanessa and Sara, too. I was too young to play. I'd get so jealous. Now I'm old enough to play. I wish we could play together.

You and Lucky should join a team.

Another good thing…Susan and John aren't getting rid of me and Eric. John said three children was their limit. So with a new baby coming, they won't be able to help another foster kid. Susan said she was sorry. She said she knows how important it is for us to be together. She said something like what Momma would say. When it pours, have faith. She said, "The sun always rises." But she also said they want to keep us. She said the choice was mine.

I told her that I'd rather be with you. But if we have to be apart, I like being there with her and

John.

It's time for dinner. I love you, Victor. Please be okay.

~Isaac

CHAPTER ELEVEN
This Place Is Not My Home

From: victory333@email.com
To: isaac-the-great@email.com
Subject: Re: I hope you're okay.

I'm okay. I'm at a county group home. I'm only here for a few days. So much has happened. The cops picked me up at the library. I was so scared. They took me to the juvenile hall. They took Boom to a kennel. I stayed in juvie for six hours. I thought for sure they'd send me away. I was ready for it. But they didn't. Finally, I have good news. The thief was caught!

Well, it wasn't really a thief. It was Boom. Confused? I was, too. This is what happened. Remember how Lucky and I set up the camera in the living room? When Lucky and I left to go back to school, the house was empty. Boom used to just bury his bones in the backyard. They weren't real bones but plastic ones. Amy forgot to buy more. She said it slipped her mind. Boom wanted to keep burying stuff.

I must have left the record out. Then Boom buried it. He buried all sorts of stuff. Brian dug up the backyard. Everything was there, including the money clip!

The caseworker said I won't be going back to Brian and Amy's. They're sending me to a different group home. The caseworker said it will be short term. She said they will work to place me as soon as possible. She also said I will have counseling. I told her I didn't need counseling.

She said it is mandatory in the group home. That means I have to.

I guess things could be worse. At least I'm not going to juvie. Especially for something I didn't do.

Remember when Dad was alive and we'd all go camping? We'd camp at the beach, usually. But one year, we camped at Lake Ming. I was ten. I was old enough to sleep in my own tent. Mom and Dad let you stay in there with me. We kept hearing scratching noises. We were scared, but we didn't want to tell Mom and Dad. We didn't want them to take us out of our tent. We toughed it out. I never told you what happened after you fell asleep.

It was late. The moon was high in the sky. Dad was snoring. The scratching started again. It got louder and louder. I couldn't take it anymore. I left the tent to investigate. I followed the sound to a nearby tree. It was a raccoon. I picked up a stick and poked at it. I was trying to scare it away.

It didn't work. The raccoon only got madder.
The raccoon started hissing at me. I thought it
was going to bite me! But Momma was there. She
had heard me. She followed me.
Momma shooed the raccoon
away. I was relieved. Momma
said I was brave. She said next
time tell her or Dad. She didn't
want me to get hurt. But she
said she loved how brave I
was.

When I left my
foster home, when I ran
away, I thought I was
being brave. But I
wasn't. I didn't feel brave in the car. I
didn't feel brave in the library. I was scared.
I ran away because I was afraid. Not because I was
brave.

I won't do that again. I promise. I won't run away because I'm afraid.

Anyway. I'm glad things are better for you. Your play is coming up! I wish I could be there to watch it. Tell me more about Katie. Have you talked to her yet? I hope so. Now *that* would be brave.

Love you,
Victor

CHAPTER TWELVE
Finally

From: isaac-the-great@email.com
To: victory333@email.com
Subject: The play was awesome!

Finally! I was worried they hauled you off to juvie. I thought they just didn't want to tell me. Now I can relax. I knew you weren't the thief. I'm relieved everyone else knows that too. But Boom? Hahaha.

I didn't see that coming. I thought for sure it was Rockford. He was so quick to blame you.

If you and Lucky hadn't set up the video…

I don't like to think about it. I'm just happy the truth came out.

I remember that camping trip. It's okay that you didn't tell me. I forgot about the noises. I miss camping. My favorite part of camping is the s'mores Momma would make. I'm craving them!

They're super-easy to make.

All you need is…

- marshmallows
- chocolate
- graham crackers

Smashed and melted in a campfire! Melted to perfection. :) How did Momma make it stay on a stick? Magic, I guess. LOL. I'm not going camping anytime soon. Especially with Susan expecting a baby. Maybe I can use the stove? I'll experiment.

To answer your question, yes. I finally spoke more than two words to Katie. Only once. I asked her if she was looking forward to the play. She said yes. She looked me straight in the eyes! My cheeks felt like they were on fire.

I'm so excited about the play. It was a lot of fun. I memorized all of my lines. I didn't get too nervous. Stephanie said I might forget the words if my nerves get me. I said, "Great! Don't tell me that."

I was worried all night. I worried my nerves were gonna get me. All that work memorizing the play would have been for nothing. But I didn't forget. I walked onto the stage. The lights were bright. The lights shone down on me. I couldn't see the people watching.

Then I said my first line. I forgot about the people watching. The story came alive. It was awesome. I wish you could have been there.

Now, Thanksgiving is around the corner. It won't be the same.

Love,

~Isaac

P.S. Susan and John celebrated Day of the Dead. They let me put up a picture of Dad. I miss him a lot.

P.P.S. How is the group home? Please let me know ASAP!

CHAPTER THIRTEEN
Not Easy

From: victory333@email.com
To: isaac-the-great@email.com
Subject: I time-traveled!

I wish I could have been there! Momma would be proud. Well, now you have to do more plays. Especially when Momma comes home. That way we all can watch.

The group home is okay. The computer is even older than the last one I used. The internet is so slow, I can't do anything. Except check and send emails. Most websites won't even load. My foster keepers at least had cell phones. Even if I didn't.

No one in this place has a cell phone. If our guards do—that's what I call the group leaders—they don't bring them into the home. We have landlines! The phone is actually connected to wires in the wall. It's like I traveled back in time! It feels like a hundred years! Or the 1990s.

Group home is okay. Other than the old, old stuff. It's a lot like Amy and Brian's. We have chores. There are a ton of rules. Lights out at 8:00 p.m. The only new thing is there are more people. And I have counseling now, too.

I had my first session yesterday. It was okay, I guess. I didn't tell her anything. She kept asking me about our parents. She asked me about Momma a lot. If I was mad at her. How I felt about her stealing all that money. I mean, how does she think I feel?! How would she feel? Of course it bothers me. Of course I'm mad at Momma. Of course I think she made a really bad choice. Anyway, I just kept quiet.

The counselor said I will have to talk with her. She said she will make the decision about me. About when I go back into a foster home. The caseworker didn't tell me that. And they wonder why I don't trust them! They want me to be honest. *They* should be honest. I'm not a little kid!

Anyway, compared to sitting in juvie, things are okay. Even if I stay in this group home until Momma gets out. But I gotta go. Lights out soon.

TTYS
Victor

P.S. I'm trying to remember what Momma said. When it pours, have faith. It's not easy.

1 Attachment
Group-home.jpg

Want to Keep Reading?

Turn the page for a sneak peek at
the next book in the series.

NOT HOME
FOR THE
HOLIDAYS

Traditions tumble.
Cookies crumble.

Nothing will
be the same.

BROTHERS

CYN BERMUDEZ

ISBN: 9781538382332

CHAPTER ONE
The First Signs of Fall

From: isaac-the-great@email.com
To: victory333@email.com
Subject: I'm making stuffing!!!!!

    Dad always cooked the turkey. Every Thanksgiving. It was the only thing he knew how to cook. But he was good at it. He made the best turkey. Remember Momma's first time?

    It was after Dad died. Our first Thanksgiving without him. Momma had the oven too hot. The turkey was burnt on the outside and

raw on the inside. Momma was so sad. She cried
a lot. I had never seen Momma cry like that.
We ended up eating at Denny's. I was fine with
that. You cheered Momma up. You gobbled like
a turkey. You made her laugh. I laughed, too.
But we also missed Dad so much. Her turkey got
better after that. She
watched a YouTube
video on how to
cook turkey.

   Now that
Momma is in
jail, will she get turkey
dinner? I hope so. I don't want her to be sad.

   I wonder how our sisters are doing. Vanessa
and Sara cried so much when the cops came.
I wish I could email them, too. Are their foster
keepers like mine or like yours? Don't be mad, but
I hope they are more like mine. Like Susan and
John. You seem to get bad ones.

I remembered to call Susan and John foster keepers! Just like you said. Not our parents. Just our keepers. Keeping us safe until it's time to go back with Momma. At least I hope. Remember, Susan is going to have a baby. The baby will be their first. I don't think she'll want me or Eric when it gets here. They haven't said anything about it. But I'm worried. I can tell Eric is worried, too. He's being extra nice.

Oh, I have something cool to tell you. Stuff you'll like. Last night, Susan told us stories about the little people. Goblins. She called them duwende. That's what they're called where she is from. She grew up in the Philippines. Her mom and dad had a farm in the country. She said little people lived there, too. They stayed mostly invisible. But they like to come out during winter. Sometimes they play pranks, too.

The duwende live out in nature. They live in trees and burrows. Sometimes, they live under rocks. Or in the small, dark places in a house. In the winter, Susan's parents built the goblins a shelter from the rain. Then the duwende would not play pranks.

John, Eric, and I are going to build a shelter here. For the duwende. John thinks Eric and I should do more together. Help us bond. Since we're both their foster kids. We're making the goblin shelter out of Popsicle sticks. I asked Susan if there are duwende here. She said yes. She said they are everywhere.

I found this site about the duwende: http://www.goblins-around-the-world.com/filipino-duwende-myth.html

Susan told us about her cousins. She said that one time they made a duwende mad. They were playing hide-and-seek. Her youngest cousin forgot to say, "Pardon me." So she got sick. The duwende cursed her cousin. Susan and her other cousins went back and offered fruit. They said,

"Please, pardon me." Then she got better. I told Susan the duwende didn't sound nice. She said only if you're not polite. I think I'm polite. I hope.

ABOUT THE AUTHOR

Cyn Bermudez is a writer from Bakersfield, California. She attended college in Santa Barbara, California, where she studied physics, film, and creative writing. Her work can be found in anthologies such as *Building Red: Mission Mars*, *The Best of Vine Leaves Literary Journal* (2014), and more. Her fiction and poetry can also be found in *Middle Planet*, *Perihelion SF*, *Strangelet*, *Mirror Dance*, *805 Literary and Art Journal*, among others. For more information about Cyn, visit her website at www.cynbermudez.com.